THE PROVIDENCE OF NEIGHBORING BODIES

Jean Ann Douglass

THE PROVIDENCE OF NEIGHBORING BODIES

OBERON BOOKS
LONDON

WWW.OBERONBOOKS.COM

First published in 2018 by Oberon Books Ltd
521 Caledonian Road, London N7 9RH
Tel: +44 (0) 20 7607 3637 / Fax: +44 (0) 20 7607 3629
e-mail: info@oberonbooks.com
www.oberonbooks.com

A catalogue record for this book is available from the British
Library.

PB ISBN: 9781786825902
E ISBN: 9781786825919

Cover: design by Christopher Calderhead,
photography by Kent Meister

eBook conversion by Lapiz Digital Services, India.

For Eric,
who knew I was a playwright before I did

and

For Alley,
who supported this play since before it was written

The Providence Of Neighboring Bodies received a workshop on 2 June 2015 at Collaborative Arts Project 21 in New York City produced by Dutch Kills Theater, Artistic Director, Alley Scott, with the following cast and creative contributors:

DORA – Kate Benson
RONNIE – Anne Gridley
JANE – Anna Abhau Elliott

Director – Jess Chayes
Design – Sara C. Walsh
Stage Manager – Tegan Ritz McDuffie

The Providence Of Neighboring Bodies had its world premiere on 23 February 2017 at Theater 511, an Ars Nova Fling, in New York City produced by Dutch Kills Theater, Artistic Director, Alley Scott, with the following cast and creative contributors:

DORA – Lori Elizabeth Parquet
RONNIE – Amy Staats
JANE – Dinah Berkeley

Director – Jess Chayes
Production Stage Manager – Allison Raynes
Scenic Design – Carolyn Mraz
Lighting Design – Derek Wright
Costume Design – Evan Prizant
Sound Design – Asa Wember
Music Composition – Chris Chappell
Properties Design – Jess Adams

The Providence Of Neighboring Bodies had its UK premiere on 3 August 2018 at Underbelly, in Edinburgh produced by Dutch Kills Theater, Artistic Director, Alley Scott, with the following cast and creative contributors:

DORA – Lori Elizabeth Parquet
RONNIE – Amy Staats
JANE – Dinah Berkeley

Director – Jess Chayes
Production Stage Manager – Allison Raynes
Scenic Design – Carolyn Mraz
Lighting Design – Derek Wright
Costume Design – Evan Prizant
Sound Design – Asa Wember
Music Composition – Chris Chappell
Properties Design – Jess Adams

Characters

DORA

RONNIE

JANE, A BEAVER

Setting
An apartment complex in North Providence, Rhode Island.

Time
Now-ish.

A note on casting
This show must not have an all-white cast.
If Jane is cast with a woman of color,
she should not be the only person of color in the cast.

A note on performance
The text in Berthold Baskerville font is directed to the
audience. While this font is used, the actors are speaking
directly to the audience, letting us in on what's going on
inside their heads. They are not acting out what they're
saying, but telling a story about a thing that is happening to
them in the present moment. DORA and RONNIE are more
confident inside the stories in their heads than they are in
the world. Their perception is not always reality.

The text in Courier New font is showing us
their external reality, and should be played
as a relatively naturalistic scene.

'Since the first colonies were settled in the Americas, the industrious, herbivorous, family-oriented beaver has been treated as a nuisance. Nearing extinction in the early 20th century, laws protecting the beaver population were put into place, and they flourished. However, the beaver's role in reshaping landscapes with dams and flooding, while effective at preventing drought and preserving land, wreaked havoc on housing built in low-lying areas. From the 1950s-1970s, Rhode Island, prevented from killing beaver by protection laws, trapped their beaver population and released them in neighboring Connecticut and Massachusetts. The state successfully eradicated beaver within its borders. While no formal beaver removal program is currently sanctioned by Rhode Island, there are still no beavers there.'

We open with morning light.

DORA: I get up in the morning without an alarm. The sun streams into my bedroom in this really beautiful way that makes this part of the day so easy. Then from there, it's over to the kitchen to put a kettle on the stove. While the water is heating up, I go for a pee, get out my foam roller, and do weight lifting with cans of soup that I keep on the counter for this very purpose.

The water boils and – ah ah ah! – I realize I forgot to grind the coffee. I do so, holding my finger on the button until the grinding changes its musical key. I am looking out the window. I do my best not to stare, even though I know she can't see me, due to the fishbowl effect and it being lighter outside than it is in my kitchen, but I am afraid it's rude to let my eyes linger too long on Ronnie, as she fusses in her balcony garden.

The coffee has been ground sufficiently for a good long time now, and I notice this with a start, and stop pressing the button. I pour the grounds into my french press, pour the water on top, slowly, allowing the coffee to bloom first. In my head I start considering what I will say when I take this press pot for two out to my balcony, notice she is there, and invite her to come sit on my respectable and only a bit outdated outdoor furniture.

I head back to the bedroom to change, and think better of it. It's Saturday. It's casual. A bathrobe is normal. A bathrobe and a fresh swipe of eyeliner and a little lip tint and some sunscreen on my décolletage.

I grab the unpressed pot, a mug – just one, I don't want to be presumptuous – and sway breezily onto the balcony, careful not to lay my eyes on Ronnie before I get there, lest it seem rude I don't already have a mug for her.

I face my apartment as I press down the press pot, thinking 'Oh, hell-*o* Ronnie!' and 'Oh! You startled me! I didn't realize you were up so early' and 'Ronnie! Hi!'

I spin around smoothly with my eyes on my hands as
I pour into my mug, and I cry 'Oh! –' and then stop,
because no one is there.

RONNIE: I run the water at the sink, filling a mason jar for the
flowers I just picked. Daisies frankly look a little stupid and
cheap like this, but I have been doing my research, and
shit like this is all the rage. Shabby chic, or whatever. Or
at least I saw this really successful host several towns over
doing this in their listing photos. So I went to Job Lot and
found a jar – well, six jars really, but the prices there are
so cheap it was better than buying one jar anywhere else –
and have been waiting for my day off to retake this photo.

Directors are always saying on the director's commentary
tracks that the light is best in the early mornings, so here
I am, up before I want to be on a Saturday, picking flowers
to put in mason jars, camera at the ready.

You know, they advertise to hosts that they'll send a
professional photographer to your place, free of charge?
Quality control, and all that. I wrote in to ask about it –
'just email us to ask about it' – and a few minutes later
they wrote back to turn me down. They need to focus
their resources on areas with great tourism potential for
the time being, and hope to be able to accommodate my
request soon.

So here I am at 7:15 on a Saturday morning, new camera
in hand. Positioning a daisy just right. Adjusting the blinds
just right.

Sighs.

Ronnie, this better fucking work.

DORA: Two cups of coffee for me then! That's fine. No big
deal. This could have been my intention all along. I do
love coffee. I've been trying to limit myself to one cup,
more than that can make me anxious, irritable, in this way
that even B vitamins can't shake me out of. But what's the
harm in it now? I already went grocery shopping for the

weekend. It's Saturday. If I get a little irritable, so what? Really. So what? Maybe sitting here on my balcony, irritable, will feel good for a change. It's good to change your perspective every once in a while, and I'm looking at All. That. Coffee…and it feels good to be bad. It feels good to think about drinking All. That. Coffee and how *sour* I'll feel. Sour and bitter like this thick, tart brew, with its grainy finish right at the end. Right when you least expect it to stick between your teeth. To coat your tongue. Muck as a final tasting note to all this pleasure. That's me. By noontime I'll be the muck. I'll coat your tongue. I'll be proud of it. I'll brag. I'll shout it from this balcony: *I AM THE MUCK! DORA IS THE MUCK!* And people in the parking lot will look up at me, but I won't even notice because I'll be too busy staring at the sky, clutching my railing to save me from blasting off like a spaceship.

I am holding my first cup, and eyeing the press pot. It's filled with all the coffee I have left to drink when this cup is done. I hardly even see the coffee in my cup, I'm so blinded by my desire for cup number two. But I stay strong and remember to savor it. I want to feel the change, notice it sip by sip.

RONNIE: It's not that it's not focused, it is. And the camera is brand new, with new batteries. I even put it on the counter to take the photo. And I know that is not the same as a tripod, but you don't need a tripod when you have counters and hardcover books. They'll always try to upsell you, but the human race got along fine without tripods for thousands of years.

No matter what I do, these pictures don't look quite right.

My students just get this stuff. The other day I was trying to show a video in my class, but instead of the video, there were all these numbers on the screen, and I had three remotes, and all of them had rows and rows of numbers and symbols, circle buttons and rectangle buttons, with textures so some of them feel different, so what, I can train to use it blindfolded? So I never need to look away from the screen?

I had to catalog how ridiculous these were, and I started to count the number of buttons on the remotes. How many of each type. How many on each remote. I needed to know.

It must have been taking me longer than I thought because one of my students asked if I was alright. I honestly couldn't tell if she cared or what but the whole class was staring at me like I was in a zoo. *Wouldn't you know it? Out of batteries.* And I walked to my desk and put the remotes in the drawer and we had silent reading time for the rest of the period.

DORA: I feel it. Ronnie should see me now, sitting here with all this power. It's radiating up from my taint to my diaphragm. My diaphragm is smiling. I bet if she came out on to her balcony right now, she'd stare at my torso and not be able to take her eyes off my smiling diaphragm. *My eyes are up here,* I'd say, and cackle, and she'd be embarrassed and meet my eyes for a second, only to have her gaze travel slowly back down, over my chin, over my clavicle, over my sternum, coming to rest on my winking, grinning diaphragm.

RONNIE: The light has already started to look like regular morning light. I regret being up so early on the weekend, and the flowers look like they'd rather be anywhere else but here. I feel guilty for picking them off my balcony. What a sad end for something approaching pretty, the way these are. What terrible flowers to make me feel like this. What asshole flowers. They don't own me. They don't deserve better than my kitchen table. I deserve better than this kitchen table – I was cum laude at a top 50 school – but these flowers are fine here. They're where they should be. This is a respectable end for them.

RONNIE: I grab them out of their vase and walk towards the balcony. Can daisies re-root? This is reversible. They're going to be fine. I'm trying to get them to stand up straight, but the stems are weak. I'm trying and trying and then I bury them so just the bloom is sticking out of the dirt. That's when I realize a voice is talking to me. I didn't notice because it's saying *yoo-hoo* and I'm not the sort of person you would yoo-hoo at unless you thought I was someone else. It's my balcony neighbor, wearing a brightly patterned robe sort of approaching a kimono, and she looks ecstatic to see me. Like this has made her whole day. Her eyes are wide and she's waving and she's saying my name, which doesn't give me the option of admitting I can never remember hers. I wave back, and smile, but don't let my lips part. If you show your teeth, your mouth is already open and then you're expected to say something. I don't know what to say.

DORA: *(Simultaneously with RONNIE.)*

Yoo-hoo!

DORA: She's there. I hear the sliding door open and close and she's there, fussing with her plants. I suck the coffee grinds out of my teeth. Make her wait, but not too long. Too long and she'll be gone.

```
Oh! Ronnie!

Hi, there!

Yoo-hoo, Ronnie!

Yoo-hoo!

Yoo-hoo, Ronnie!

Yoo-hoo!

Yoo-hoo, Ronnie!
```

And then it happens. Our eyes meet. She hasn't noticed my diaphragm yet, but boy, it is smiling so hard my breasts have perked up with the edges of its grin. She is smiling, too. On her face. And her hand is waving back. At me.

```
It's Dora.
```

I stop her before she has a chance to stumble. I don't care, this always happens.

```
Don't worry, this always happens. Every
time I go to Starbucks they write Laura on
my cup. Even if I stand there repeating
DORA. DOR-AHH as they're writing. They
think they're doing it right. If I can
be honest with you, sometimes I give my
name out as Laura at restaurants, it saves
the disappointment, theirs and mine. It's
best not to make them feel guilty right
as they're calling your name for a table,
they've just done you a huge favor and
so why make them feel bad? And I know,
I'm not doing myself any favors by giving
out the wrong name at a restaurant, but
really, I only do it if I'm traveling,
```

16

never around here, since it would be so
embarrassing if anyone knew who I was,
and corrected me on my own name. Can you
imagine? Besides, it's not like I have
occasions to go to restaurants around here
that much, what do I have to celebrate I
mean really, so it's not a decision I need
to make very often. So yes, it's Dora, not
Laura or Cora or Flora. Speaking of flora,
you're planting in your garden!

The words are just coming and coming and my heart is
beating faster and faster and I feel myself free-associating
with everything in my field of vision. Parking lot. Telephone
pole. Hill that hides the water treatment facility. Balcony.
Stop light. Awning. Gas station. Ronnie. Ronnie. Ronnie.

RONNIE: She doesn't want much company in her
conversation, Dora. I'm smiling, at the appropriate times,
nodding, occasionally, and each time I do, she gets a new
burst and goes. We get to a point where I don't know why
I'm still standing here. I didn't think it was possible to
stand here this long in a conversation and not say anything,
but I've done it.

And here we both are.

And it seems to strike us both at the same moment – just
how long it's been since this started, me, mutely twitching
my face and bobbing my head pleasantly, and Dora, not
showing any signs of coming up for air, and when it strikes
us, maybe it's the look on my face, which makes her realize
– but she just stops talking, abruptly, and we're silent, just
looking at each other, just silent with this WHAT ARE WE
DOING face on, and whatever it is, it is just. so. FUNNY.

So. FUNNY.

And I'm crying, I'm doubled over, and so is Dora. And she
offers something like an apology, which is even funnier, and
I start to say something, but it just comes out as a snort.

DORA: I knew we'd be friends. I mean, what are the odds, two women, around our age, adjoining balconies, in this town, of course we should be friends. It's just so obvious. I'm always having great ideas like this. And I think probably most people have great ideas, but what sets me apart, what really, truly sets me apart is gumption. I take initiative. I am resourceful. And spirited.

RONNIE: I open my door, head inside, and come back before she's had a chance to stop laughing.

```
Here.
```

I toss her a can of Coors. It's the first thing I've managed to say to her, and she seems a little shocked. Or maybe shocked to have me toss a beer to her over our balcony railings. It sails over my railing, over the eight inch gap to the lot below, over her railing, and she catches it like anyone catches anything they weren't expecting: a little fumbly, and not quite preventing it from smashing her boob.

```
Don't act like it's too early. It would be
rude to let me drink alone.
```

I pop the tab, and she hesitates for a moment and does the same. I raise my can in her direction and then put it to my mouth. I take a big gulp, maybe two, and I am just letting the day go away. I'm giving up on it. Today wanted something different from me than I wanted from it, and here I am, letting the day have its way with me. Letting twelve ounces of Coors put me in my place. This is me not trying to fight it anymore. I'm happier this way. I'm present. On my damn balcony, with this cold beer and my weird neighbor, and we are drinking. We're just drinking.

I let the can come down, and she's taking little sips. Little, quick sips, with a flash of a smile between each one.

DORA: I love cheap beer. It's too early to tell Ronnie, but this is my favorite beer, and I couldn't be happier that Coors, of all things, is what she tossed at me, across our balcony railings, way too early in the day to be drinking. I went through a phase, of pretending to like all the froo-froo beers. But it's just so much work. I like to think that you can just get to a point, this point we all should get to, where you stop pretending you don't like Coors. Where you find other people who have also stopped pretending they don't like Coors. And we can take all that effort we all put into pretending we were fancier people than we are, and channel it into being alive, and all of our past foibles will become these funny old stories we tell to each other about how silly things used to be.

RONNIE: Of all the people in the world, Dora would not be my first or second choice drinking buddy. But there's this thing about proximity. This thing like summer camp, where you find yourself next to a person, and it's like, why not this person? Why the hell not? And it becomes confusing why you wouldn't have them in your top one or two drinking buddies, because it's a person, and they're there. And they have the same balcony as you do, just a few feet over, so you stop imagining some circumstance where things are better than this, and you realize that things ARE this, and that whole realization doesn't even take place because you just become comfortable with where you are.

And I'm Ronnie. And this is my neighbor Dora. And this is now my second Coors.

DORA: You can spend your whole life planning things, run-ins where someone works, what you're wearing when it happens, but what I like about planning is that it opens you up to surprises. Surprising yourself by drinking on an empty stomach with your neighbor who is probably going to be your new best friend.

My press pot is sitting here, empty and forgotten, and I'm enjoying the way the beer is playing with the coffee inside my body. Where there were gushing rivers, dams have been put up, and my body is becoming an ecosystem with a wall of pent up energy allowing a steady falls to pour over the top, where it collects in introspective pools and evaporates up into my brain making me giddy with the possibility of upcoming downpours.

Oh, why not? I don't have anywhere to be.

RONNIE: What else would a person do around here on a Saturday, anyhow?

DORA: We toss aside formalities as we toss aside our empty cans.

RONNIE: I guess part of me is genuinely asking.

DORA: I'm telling stories.

RONNIE: I've never really figured out what to do around here on a Saturday.

DORA: I grew up in this town. In a house down the street.

RONNIE: The movie theater is a little far, and it's probably not good for me to spend all that daytime in the dark.

DORA: This town that's the smallest town in the smallest state, with more nail salons per capita than anywhere in America.

RONNIE: But I guess that's why we invented books and balconies, right?

DORA: When I was a kid, things were really different around here, you know? My mom used to tell me to stay away from this apartment complex, do you believe that? She always said there was an 'undesirable element' over here. And I guess there was, before they covered that reservoir across the street with all the grass. If you just leave water out, uncovered like that, you're going to have some...

RONNIE: Some what? What / would that do?

DORA: I mean that's what she always said. I don't know how true it is, but there's got to be some truth to it, it's not like she just made it up. But times have changed since then, I mean, look who lives here now. Me. You.

RONNIE: 'Undesirable' doesn't sound too far off.

DORA: And honestly, undesirable? What a way to describe… Everyone is desirable to someone, it's just how the world works, I think. And it's really a misuse of the word, undesirable, if there's a group together, they can't feel that way among themselves. It's unfair, really.

RONNIE: Who really understands words, anyway? I'm an English teacher and I use words I don't understand. I mean, I think I understand them, but I know enough to know I'm just getting it all wrong all the time.

I read more than I talk to people. Always have. I pronounce things wrong all the time, too, I'm sure of it. The thing is, I'm usually talking to my students, and they don't know how it's supposed to be pronounced, either, and I have this position of authority. I'm their teacher. And I've probably trained hundreds of kids to say words the wrong way, but what can I do about it? I don't even know which words I pronounce wrong, so where could I even start tracking them down and giving them the correct information and making amends for what I've done to them? I don't even fully understand what I've done to them, and that's the worst part.

If I were a better teacher I could probably figure out how to get a job somewhere where the pay is decent. You know, I've been trying to rent my couch out on the internet? Hell, I'll give them the bed and sleep on the couch myself at this point. I can't afford to be proud. But no one has ever even tried to book me. And I keep trying to make it look better online, but I'm just fooling myself, really. No one is ever going to want to visit here. They can all get their nails done and visit a strip mall in their own towns. But what am I going to do, you know? I don't have much else to offer.

I thought that by the time I was this age, with my good government job, I'd be able to look in the future, and be like, there, that spot, that's where I'll be able to not rush to the bank as soon as I get a paycheck to deposit. That's where I'll have a hammock.

You want another beer?

DORA: We're in sync. She tosses another beer to me. But this time, the sweat from her hand is mixing with the sweat of the can and it hooks where it shouldn't, and goes over her railing, at an angle where it misses MY railing, and sails straight through my outstretched fingers and over the corner of her balcony and out into the parking lot. I cover my face because I can't bear to see what happens next, while Ronnie rushes forward and throws out her arm in a jazz hand, though the can is so far beyond her reach and I am peeking through my fingers at Ronnie trying to jam both fists in her mouth and her eyes are bugging out, and right when we see the inevitable, we both duck down on our balconies just in time to hear the smash of glass as the can goes through the windshield of a car.

RONNIE: I scurry into my apartment. When I get in, I start to close the blinds, then realize that closing them would look suspicious. I am not suspicious. I'm a normal person who lives her life and can't afford to break other people's things. Who wouldn't break other people's things because I'm a nice schoolteacher that students don't hate and parents don't mind, and destruction of property is not something on my résumé.

I should do nothing. The unsuspicious person does nothing, and I did not do this. So I will take a nap. When they come knocking, I'll need to be roused from my bed and my hair will be terrible, and they'll say 'oh, sorry, ma'am, we didn't mean to wake you. We were wondering if you had seen any of this beer throwing incident that happened earlier, but you were clearly sleeping, so we are so sorry to bother you, especially after you just managed to sleep through the sound of a windshield being smashed by a beer can, and here we go and ruin it and wake you up!' And I'll remember to look concerned about the windshield, and worried for my own car, maybe clutching at my robe, and they'll say 'no, no, ma'am, not to worry. We have the owner downstairs, so I'm sure your vehicle is fine. Just fine.' And they'll leave feeling guilty for having caused me any stress, and I will go back to my nap.

DORA: I duck into my apartment like a fox, or a meerkat, or whatever animal is best known for ducking into places. And I – wooosh! – close the blinds, and I am closed in, I'm safe. But what about Ronnie? I walk over and touch the wall that connects our two apartments. We can't be together right now, I know she knows this, but it's hard for her. Inside that tough exterior, she's more sensitive than she looks.

I have to reassure her. I sit down on my carpet next to the air vent our apartments share. I start whispering to her. This is what girls do. This is what best friends who share a wall do when they're in trouble. I know she must be worried about what will happen now. She's sure to be on the other side, waiting to hear from me. I tell her not to turn herself in. I tell her no one saw, but me, and I wouldn't tell a soul. I tell her that everything is going to be okay, because it is. I tell her that our friendship will not only survive this, but will be stronger because of it. I tell her I'm so glad this finally happened, and it's so much better than I'd ever imagined. I tell her it's our little secret and what a fun day I'm having and that we should meet back out there in a few hours when this all has blown over. She's so scared she's not saying anything, but I want to tell her so many things. I curl up on the floor and whisper to her until I fall asleep.

RONNIE: I wake up and it's dark. I'm on my couch, and I'm fully dressed and I don't know if it's Saturday night or Sunday morning, or if I've slept all the way into the future, and there are flying cars now. Time has passed and no one is knocking on my door, so maybe everything is fine. Maybe it's not as bad as I thought it might be. I sit up. My head hurts. I'm sure it's fine if I go out to the balcony and just look. There's nothing suspicious about walking out to your own balcony in the dark. Nothing at all suspicious.

I walk over and slide open the door. I step out onto the balcony. Turn. Slide the door closed behind me. I make like I'm going to check out my daisies, and that's when I see them. Police cars. They're blocking off the parking lot, and we are barricaded in, and yellow tape is blocking off the area. Little tents with numbers on them are next to pieces of broken glass, and there's one plainclothes person in this sea of police officers. He's wearing a robe. He's talking loudly with his hands, but I can't make out any sound. He is pointing, wildly, in every direction.

I go back inside before anyone can see me, and walk to the kitchen and pour myself a huge glass of water. My head is pounding, and my heart is racing, and I need to clear my head and think.

DORA: What a rush! I'm feeling very clever. I think Ronnie will be so impressed. What a day! What a day we're having.

It wasn't Ronnie that threw the can of beer. Oh no.
It couldn't have been. Someone's already taken credit.
We're not the undesirable element.

They're going to find a note. The note will keep her safe.

RONNIE: I don't know what to do. My mind is racing, so I
do what I always do when situations fail me. I open my
computer and check my email.

I have a message. It's a woman named Jane who wants to
rent my couch. Tonight.

JANE: Hello! I know it's short notice, but
I would like to come to your town late
tonight. I use this site all the time
– please check out my reviews – and I'm
willing to pay extra because of the
inconvenience of my late arrival. I look
forward to meeting you! Jane.

RONNIE: Finally! It seems like eons ago that I first put the
listing up! Oh my god, this is such perfect timing. No,
this is horrible timing! The police are swarming, the
parking lot is blocked off. I check the clock. Nine P.M.
Okay. If she's willing to pay me extra for a late arrival,
it will probably be hours until she arrives. I can figure out
something by then.

Dear Jane. A late arrival is fine, just let
me know roughly when to expect you.

And thanks for choosing my listing!

Ha! I'm on a damn cloud.

Accept request.

JANE: Dear Ronnie. That's excellent news.
It'll take me about two hours to get down
there. Thanks for being so accommodating,
Jane.

RONNIE: It's almost eleven. The apartment has never looked better. I put the daisies back on the table. The pillows are fluffed. There are fresh sheets on the pullout couch, already pulled out, saving Jane the trouble before she goes to bed.

I make a cup of tea and wander out to the balcony, like it's something I do. Most of the police cars have gone and the ones that are left don't even have their flashing lights on. The cops are doing a lot of chatting and leaning on cars and I'm too far away to tell, but I'm sure there are doughnuts involved. They seem to be losing steam, and they might even be gone by the time Jane arrives.

I don't want to fall asleep before she gets here. I move to the kitchen table with my tea, jittering my leg to stay awake. I honestly don't even think I like tea, and never had any in the house until I started worrying about stocking my kitchen for hosting guests. Let's face it, guests like you better if you have things for them. Like tea. Face cloths. Seashell soaps or whatever. So I bought some stupid tea. And it's probably good I'm finally having some, so the box will be open and a packet missing and Jane won't feel awkward about whether or not she should be the first one to open a brand new box of tea. 'I was going to make some tea, but this box isn't open. Is it special tea? Are you saving it for something? Oh. I can't believe you bought tea just for me. I don't even like peppermint, I was just being polite.'

DORA: Written words have a lot of power. My words have power when I say them, of course, but when I write them down, it just sets things in motion. Things you couldn't expect. I can keep words in my head all day, and become accustomed to them not doing much of anything. They're not achieving their full potential until I write them down and put them out in the world.

I try not to do it too often. It's risky. But I saw Ronnie's face. She was so scared. She doesn't have anyone else to protect her. But I'm here.

I sit and focus on the note, sitting under the windshield wiper. In my mind's eye, I see it getting found. It getting read. The bewilderment and the ensuing hunt. She will be protected.

RONNIE: Shit! The buzzer is buzzing. I hop up too fast and I'm shaking the hot tea from my hand as I answer,

Hello?

JANE: Hi, it's Jane, just got in so sorry I'm late!

RONNIE: No trouble. Third floor.

I buzz her up. It's here.

It's happening.

She's here.

She's coming up the stairs.

Oh shoot, I can't believe I'm letting her carry all her bags on her own, but what choice do I have now? Dammit, it's too late. She could take either stairwell, so if I go to help her now, I'll only have a 50/50 chance of actually running into her, so that ship seems to have sailed. And also, maybe she'd be offended if I offered, like a woman traveling alone can't carry her bags. If she brought her bags all the way here to begin with, what's a couple of flights of stairs? Right?

Three knocks.

Coming!

I say, but I don't come. I'm frozen and I have panic inside my chest and I close my eyes and mentally check around the whole apartment and see that everything is in its place and I relax a little and let myself exhale, and I walk over to the door.

I open it for Jane, and her appearance takes the breath out of me.

It's just for a moment. I think it was just for a moment, but she doesn't seem to notice and I am almost sure I'm still gracious.

I welcome her and step aside and see that at least she didn't bring anything much with her. So at least there's that. I saved myself that embarrassment.

She's smiling and I'm smiling back and I'm showing my teeth, but I'm talking, I have to talk, it's my home, and she comes in and it's so pleasant and she asks where things are and what time do I get up in the morning and how to start the coffee maker if she gets up first, and if she should make extra coffee. Then she stretches wide, with both paws in the air, and gives a big yawn, and I suggest we turn in.

JANE: I'm running a bit later than I'd like when I arrive at Ronnie's place, but she's super nice about it. You can tell how a host is actually going to treat you when you screw up something like your arrival time right off the bat. And she only looks a little weirded out when she opens the door. It's pretty par for the course, and this town of all towns, I didn't know what to expect from everyone.

It was a different story out in the parking lot. A few police cars were out there, and I felt eyes on me from when I got off the bus until I got to the front door.

Her home doesn't have much in the way of decoration, but it smells like tea and artificial pine trees. The lighting at night is pretty terrible, and doesn't do this apartment any favors. But Ronnie seems great and I see the big sliding doors that lead out to what must be the balcony I saw in the photos. With the daisies. Tomorrow, we'll have some real sunlight and I can get to work.

RONNIE: The next morning, I wake up much earlier than usual, and my apartment already smells like coffee. I start to head out to the living room, but ugh I can't be in my pajamas in front of Jane. I throw on jeans and a shirt and head out to the living room. The couch is already perfectly folded up, sheets neatly stacked in one corner. In the kitchen, there is half a pot of coffee, and a bowl covered with a tea towel, with a note next to it that explains that this is pancake batter with walnuts that Jane brought from her home in Massachusetts. 'To make some pancakes, use butter and a griddle with a spatula, in the usual way.'

I never thought hosting people could be this nice! I pour myself a coffee and start on these pancakes. Heating the pan. Melting some butter. Pouring out batter in measured cups. As the pancakes start cooking I wonder where Jane went. The bathroom is empty. The couch is empty. I look through the blinds out to the balcony and she is there, pounding away at her laptop, half-eaten plate of pancakes next to her. I want to say good morning and thank you, but don't want to interrupt whatever has her focused like that, so I tiptoe back to the kitchen and flip my pancake.

DORA: When I wake up on Sunday morning, I throw on my robe, slip into my slippers, and head to my front door. I open it, and there it is, swollen tight in its snug plastic sleeve, the Sunday Paper. I look both ways down the hall to make sure no one saw me grinning. The coast is clear, but I rearrange my face into a sleepy grimace just in case and I grab the paper and head inside.

I'm going to enjoy this. I leave the paper on the table while I get the coffee together. I'll enjoy it even more with a press pot on my balcony. What's life if you don't take all the opportunities you get to maximize your enjoyment? What's the point of it all?

With my left hand clutching the handle of the press pot and a mug, I pick up the paper with my right hand and walk towards the sliding doors. When I get there, I tuck the paper under my left armpit, so I have my right hand free to open the door. I open it, step outside, turn around to shut it, and walk over to my cafe table.

And that's when I see it. On Ronnie's balcony. A beaver is there. Eating pancakes and working on her laptop like it's her balcony.

I'm back inside in a flash. It's not safe. That beaver is much too close to Ronnie. I'm not protecting her after all.

No. A beaver isn't here. There are beavers lots of places, but not inside Ronnie's apartment. Not on Ronnie's balcony, eating pancakes.

I sit down on my couch and exhale all the air out of me and rub my eyes and consider the possibility that my brain is playing tricks on me. That's not a beaver. I was just rude to my new friend Ronnie out there. Instead of saying hi, I just ran in and slammed the door, and what will she think? What will she think of our friendship if I run inside when I notice she's on her balcony? That's not what friends do. Certainly not friends who have been through what we've been through.

I need to go back. I need to apologize. I take a deep breath and plunge my press pot and pour myself a cup of coffee, tighten the belt on my robe, and head out to the balcony with just my mug.

Good morning, Ronnie!

I say. And the beaver swivels around and says,

JANE: Oh, hi! I think Ronnie's still sleeping. My name's Jane. I'm staying on her couch for a bit.

DORA: She smiles at me. And gives her paw a wave. And I'm frozen. I'm frozen to the spot. I'm just looking into her eyes with this dead smile plastered on and time is going by, and she starts looking concerned, but I don't know what to say, and she seems to notice this, and it freezes her, too. She is also still smiling but I start to see fear welling up behind her eyes, and it's all my fault, all of it. So I blurt,

Goodness. I don't know how I mistook you for Ronnie. I mean. There aren't a lot of similarities. I just thought she'd be the one... Well, it's nice to meet you... Jane.

My name is Dora. I live here, next door to Ronnie. I usually always know what's going on over here, she's a dear friend.

JANE: Oh, how nice! She didn't mention anything about being friends with a neighbor, but this is great. It's nice to meet you, too, Dora.

DORA: Oh, that's so strange she didn't mention me. I live just next door. I have this balcony here, you see. One right over from hers. We talk out here in the mornings, which is why I wasn't expecting to see you here. In Ronnie's chair. Where she was yesterday morning.

So, Jane, what made you come back here? I mean, how did you get here? I mean, what brings you to town?

JANE: I'm doing a bit of a project where I look up my ancestors and visit their old stomping grounds. Right now I'm working on my grandfather, Oakleaf. He actually spent some time around here as a young man, believe it or not. He was a bit of a rabble rouser, or so my family likes to say. I found some of his old journals and it looks like he really got up to some shenanigans around here.

This... looks a lot different than what I was expecting, but I think I can imagine what it must have been like for him. I'm headed out soon to see more of his old haunts.

DORA: And at this point, Jane looks wistfully down at the parking lot, up to the traffic whizzing by, the telephone poles with more wires than I can count strung between them. She seems to be noticing something that I can't see, or taking comfort from these sights like they're old friends. I feel like I'm witnessing something private, something sacred and personal, and I'm scared that she'll realize I've been here the whole time and that I'm intruding on her personal thoughts and she'll, she'll, I don't know. I don't know what beavers are like.

She seems comfortable so far, and she seems to like me, which is great, I just don't know where she expects things to go from here. And I don't want to push this conversation into somewhere uncomfortable, for her, you know? I want to say normal things, but I just keep thinking *beaver* and then *don't say beaver* and I know that I'm talking, but I don't know what I'm saying because my whole brain is wrapped up trying to stop me from blurting it out.

Well, I'm sure it's not impossible to be
happy here. We have some nice restaurants.
But I don't know if —

And, I mean, there's Notte Park, which has
some woods, with trees…

JANE: Oh.

DORA: …you know, if restaurants aren't really
your cup of tea.

JANE: That sounds lovely. Thank you, Dora.
I've got some thinking to do now about the
rest of my day, but thanks for the chat.
And the tips. Maybe I'll see you later?

DORA: She smiles at me and it's so friendly but also really clear that this conversation is over. She cups her coffee mug in both …hands and stands at the railing, looking out and taking it all in.

I head back inside and sit down at the vent. Our vent, me and Ronnie.

Good morning, Ronnie,

I whisper, so just she can hear.

So much has happened.

I sip my coffee. I hear something sizzling on the stove next door, so I sit and wait for Ronnie to finish making breakfast.

RONNIE: After breakfast, I brush my hair really well and throw on some tinted chapstick. I really feel like running some errands. After those pancakes I'll have to cook up something local and special for lunch. Actually, she must have plans for the day so I should probably just plan on dinner. Let her have some adventures and we can debrief over some hearty local something.

I'm going to go to the fancy deli. I'm going to splurge on that eggplant parm I love. And then I'm going to drive over to Pawtucket – because let's face it, there are no decent wine stores over here – and I'll get some chianti to go with it. Actually, rewind a second, it'll probably be better to do that the other way around since the traffic on Mineral Spring is so unpredictable and I don't want to be driving around with eggplant in my car all day. And on the way, I'm going to stop in a few different Dunkin Donuts and make sure I run into everyone that there is to run into. It's a three coffee Sunday. I'll get smalls. I won't overdo it and the coffee will still be hot when I get to the bottom.

As I'm heading out of the apartment, I stick my head out onto the balcony.

Hi. Hey. Jane. Sorry to bother you,

I say,

but I'm headed out to get the stuff to make eggplant tonight. I need to pay you back for those pancakes with something! Dinner around eight, if you're not busy. Do you want anything else while I'm out?

RONNIE: Jane smiles warmly, and no, she doesn't need anything, and she's so happy I loved the breakfast and she'll be heading out soon and thanks again for letting her stay, it's such a comfortable pull-out.

JANE: *(Simultaneously.)* No, I don't need anything. Awesome, you liked it!

The couch was super comfy.

RONNIE: I won't bother you again until dinner, I promise.

And she waves me off with an oh-it's-no-problem gesture, and gratefully gets back to her laptop. I close the sliding door and grab my keys and head out to my car.

DORA: I see Ronnie's car pull out of the parking lot before she had a chance to come talk to me, but I can't pull myself away from the vent. Jane's presence next door has me stuck to the spot. It's all of the sounds I hear Ronnie make, shower running, dishes clinking in the sink, but I can tell it's Jane because it all has a different rhythm. It's softer, somehow. I can't tell if it's the fur on her hands deadening the sounds, or a natural gentleness, or extra care because she's moving through someone else's home.

I become a little addicted to listening to her move through the apartment. It's familiar noises, but they're so strange. I close my eyes and try to picture her. She's different than I would have expected, carefully attending to Ronnie's home. I wasn't expecting the precision. The purposefulness. I'm taking the sounds she's making and matching them with the image of her that I have in my head and I start to imagine how she handles things. She's putting down dishes just so. She's turning doorknobs gently with her paws. I find myself wanting to watch her do these things, picturing how she moves through the world. How does she hold her cellphone? Does she use her knife in the European fashion or the American?

RONNIE: The first stop is the Dunkin on Smith. It's not the closest one to my house, but it's guaranteed to have some co-workers there. Usually, I drive through one of the two drive-thrus, but today I park, and go inside. I'm right – two co-workers are in line and the vice-principal is sitting in a booth with someone whose back is to me. I start trying to catch their eyes.

I see Sarah from the social studies department notice me and I am about to wave and then it hits me that I don't really have anything to brag about.

'Great news, I have a beaver staying with me, and don't freak out, they're very friendly! I was surprised, too. But I had an open mind and it's paying off. Really helps with rent, having strangers on your couch. Ha! Ha!'

They wouldn't understand. I never tell them anything about my weekends, so why start now? But I'm already in this line and people have seen me. I make like I was looking at the menu and not at Sarah, like I don't know how much a small coffee is or whatever, and I twitch like my phone just vibrated in my pocket, and reach in, grab it, look at the blank screen and let my eyes go wide like it's someone important, hit a button and say 'hello?' as I step out of line and head outside.

I'm back in my car, and I stop my fake call mid-sentence, shoving my phone back in my pocket and starting up my car to head through the drive-thru.

JANE: I'm on foot. I've never much believed in personal vehicles. Buses are fine by me. Trains. Ferries. I wish I didn't have a fear of bicycles, because they seem like a great idea. Grandpa always said you can learn a lot about the world by walking through it. For me, I don't think it's philosophical so much as I just really like walking.

I made a map this morning. It's the best I could do based on his journal and the historic map of the town I found online, compared with the map of how it looks now. His old apartment, the diner he worked at washing dishes, before he got fired, and the community center where he volunteered and gave his lectures.

After a few hundred feet of walking, the sidewalk just sort of stops. I look up ahead and all the way up to the bend in the road, there's no more sidewalk. A car goes past, and even from this last ledge of sidewalk, it feels like it's going too fast. It's too close.

RONNIE: I stick more or less to my plan. I use drive-thrus instead of going in. Chianti first, then eggplant. I can hold this in. I'll have more to talk about with people after dinner, anyhow. I use the time to think of good conversation starter questions and I keep imagining what she'll say. I don't have a lot of stories, but I can be a good listener. I'm sure a traveler appreciates a good listener, or what are all of their adventures for?

The lines are long, the parking lots are packed. This is why I never go to the nice markets on the weekends, but I am not going to serve Jane a salad from a bag.

I've decided we'll stay inside and keep the blinds closed, and it'll just be a fun night for us. I'll be able to tell everyone about what she's like and prepare them for her. It's not like I'm some sort of hero, but I can lay a little groundwork with people before we start taking evenings out on the balcony, on full display and fully backlit. I can spread the word, once I have a few stories.

JANE: I'm waiting for a break in the traffic. It's still mid-morning, so the cars are coming at a pretty regular clip. The safest thing to do, when there's no sidewalk, is to walk against the traffic. But there's that bend up ahead. There's no way a driver would see me until after the bend.

I'm waiting it out. I'm standing, counting cars. Timing them, how many this five minutes, is it less than how many the last five minutes? The next driver that comes around the corner – number thirteen in her time block – locks eyes with me. She doesn't look away, and slows down and comes to a stop. The passenger window moves down a few inches and she asks if I'm lost. No, I say. She hasn't seen me before. I'm visiting, I say. Visiting family? Well, in a sense. I laugh. She doesn't laugh, and I go to explain the joke but in that moment she locks her doors and drives away, the passenger window snapping up as she goes.

DORA: Fur is so warm, I bet a chilled riesling would really hit the spot at the end of the day. Really spur the internal cooling system. Watch the sun go down, drink something icy as it gets dark.

But I also look at her and think of ski lodges. Of leather couches and sitting close for warmth. Maybe a red would suit. Or kahlua. Can she drink milk?

Red actually seems right. Not a pinot, though. Something spicy and super foreign. A malbec might do it. Wait. No. Shiraz. She's a shiraz.

JANE: The cars are now a safe distance away. The bush does a nice job of muffling the traffic, and I've got a warm little spot in some dead leaves and pine needles. I take my journal out of my bag, this is a really lovely spot for journaling. Maybe it's better to connect to the ground that Oakleaf walked on, rather than trudge around all day. Pencil out. Deep breath. This is what you came here for, Jane. It's fine.

DORA: In the late afternoon, the sliding door to Ronnie's balcony opens and closes. It's the cue I've been waiting for, and I go out onto my own balcony with two glasses and a bottle of red wine.

Jane?

No one ever remembers my name, I know. It's…

JANE: Dora. Right?

DORA: It's Dora, actually. Oh. Yes. You were right. Dora. That's right. How strange. Really, no one ever…

JANE: I can head inside if you need some privacy.

DORA: What?

JANE: *(Indicating the bottle.)* Your date. It's no trouble!

DORA: My… oh! This? Haha. No, there's no date. I'm in for the night, just me. This glass… I was actually coming out here to ask if you wanted to join me. I shouldn't drink this whole bottle myself, and it really doesn't keep, I don't care what anyone says, and it was so interesting what you were saying this morning about your travels? So if I'm not interrupting maybe I could hear more about it in exchange for half of this?

JANE: I accept the wine glass, and Dora's generous pour, and she leans towards me over the railing, and I don't know what I could possibly tell her about my day. I think I got some writing done. It's probably just trash, though. I start asking questions before she can get started. Like, what's with all the nail salons? Why do people drive so fast on this road?

Why does that hill across the street have a barbed wire fence around it?

DORA: Oh, that? That's not really a hill. That's the highest point in town, and that's where the town keeps the water. Instead of a water tower, you know? They planted grass over it to make it safe. And less of an eyesore, I guess. And it's covered now, so we don't get a lot of… there's less undesir- I haven't seen another beaver here in a long time.

I'd be so embarrassed if that was the most exciting thing you saw in town!

JANE: Just curious, is all.

DORA: I hope I'm not keeping you from plans with Ronnie. I just noticed the hour, and that she's not back. It's not like her.

JANE: Oh, she mentioned something about fixing dinner. Eggplant, does that sound right? She might still be at the market, we could have her buy enough that you can join us.

DORA: I wouldn't want to intrude.

JANE: I'm the one intruding, you guys are the friends here.

DORA: OK! You convinced me! I'll call her! What's her number?

RONNIE: The eggplant is hot and fresh from the market, sitting on the passenger seat. I think if I had this eggplant for the first time, I'd want to extend my trip and just hang out and eat and eat.

I turn into the complex at 7:50, and there's Jane, on the balcony, on full display. Dora has her hand on her shoulder, and her head thrown back in laughter.

I told her dinner was at eight. She agreed. That's not the plan. This is our night.

I get inside, and they're still out there. I yell out something about 'not feeling well' and 'don't mind me' and walk straight into my room without really looking outside. I'm still holding the good eggplant from Shore's and I sit down on my bedroom floor, open the foil container and eat it with my fingers.

DORA: It's a shame Ronnie isn't feeling well. We could split the bottle of wine between the three of us! It's her guest, after all. But I'd be lying if I didn't admit to myself that I was enjoying this. Enjoying having Jane's attention all to myself. Having her answer only my questions. Being the person shaping her second night in town.

I'm sure Ronnie appreciates this. Her two best friends having a great time. There's nothing worse than friends not getting along. I bet she's lying in her bed, safe, warm, hearing us laugh, grateful she brought us into her life.

Tomorrow night, I'll show Jane around. I'll take her to the billiard hall that girl I went to high school with opened a few years back and she'll hook us up with a free second round. I'll be the person walking in with a stranger, and everyone will stare and wonder where we met. Jane will be surprised at how good I am at pool. She'll wonder what else I'm good at. Just this, I'll reply. And smile. It's my only hidden talent.

JANE: Red wine makes me sleepy, and this bottle is gone. I tell Dora that I had a great time talking to her, and that I'm going to turn in. I say I don't want to be noisy with Ronnie sick in bed, but if I'm being honest with myself, I don't want to get around to talking about my day. I hand her back the wine glass, pat her elbow, rub my nose on hers, and head inside, where I make pancakes for dinner with the leftover batter.

RONNIE: In the morning, I hear Jane up early, again. She's rustling around in the kitchen, making the conspicuous noise of a person who is trying to be quiet. No matter, it's Monday and I have to go to work today.

There's still a bag from the grocery store resting against my closet door. I ate all the eggplant so it wouldn't go bad and I wouldn't have to go to the fridge to put it away. I get up and tie the bag in a tight knot, depositing it in the trash next to my bedside table, where it joins some Q-tips and cotton balls. I open my closet and find something appropriate and get dressed in the near-dark. I pull on my good boots and run a brush through my hair and head out to the kitchen.

RONNIE: Jane smiles at me and whispers 'good morning!' and gestures towards a seat at the table.

JANE: *(Simultaneously with RONNIE.)* Good morning!

JANE: Have a seat, I hope you have time for breakfast before work.

RONNIE: There are some branches of flowering shrub on the table, overshadowing the little daisies I had put out the other day. The kitchen smells like warm berries and Jane is happily fussing at the stove. I pull out my chair to sit down and there's a knock at the door. Five.

Five. Hard. Knocks.

Boom. Boom. Boom. Boom. Boom.

I am startled and Jane is startled and we're wide-eyed staring at each other and at the door, and at each other, and at the door.

I have the realization that I'm the one that lives here and I yell

Coming!

and I look at Jane for help, but she just looks confused. My feet are stuck to the floor, but I somehow walk over to the front door. Through the peephole I see two police officers. They know I'm there. They call me 'ma'am' and say they just have a few questions. They're trying to seem friendly.

I open the door and say something ridiculous like, what seems to be the trouble, officers? They ask if I noticed the commotion in the parking lot the other day.

They ask if anyone else is home. Do I live alone. I say that yes I live alone and they ask if it's true that there was a beaver on my balcony last night. Neighbors reported seeing a beaver. I stammer and am unsure what I'm saying but it's all 'website' and 'couch' and 'she has great reviews' and they're having meaningful looks at each other I have shame caught in my throat.

RONNIE: They want to talk to Jane and she just comes right over, she's heard the whole thing. She's smiling and ready to be helpful and they're holding up a photocopy of a handwritten note and asking her why she wrote it, why she stayed at the scene of the crime. Jane is calm, firm and 'there are lots of beavers' and 'you can't think that's me just because it's signed by a beaver' and 'I have rights' but all four of us know that there are no other beavers anywhere around here and it looks bad. Very bad.

JANE: *(Simultaneously with RONNIE.)*

There are lots of beavers. You can't think that's me just because it's signed by a beaver. I have rights!

DORA: I have my Monday morning paper out on my balcony. It's breezy and the paper is rustling and I have my feet up and things just don't get better than this. They don't. Who has a better time than I do? Nobody.

There is a flutter of activity next door as Ronnie – hi, Ronnie! You look like you're feeling better. Are you feeling better? – comes out to her balcony and looks over the ledge. She looks anxious. I look where she's looking and after a few moments I see a police officer walk out of the building. Then Jane. Then a police officer.

What's… I don't… Ronnie? What's going on?

She turns to me and tells me that Jane's been arrested. The police found a note signed by a beaver next to the smashed windshield. A beaver took credit.

RONNIE: There's nothing we can do, Dora.

DORA: There's nothing we should do. They found their beaver.

I want to tell her that I did it all for her. The note. I want Ronnie to be safe. I want us to be safe on our balconies and safe to enjoy this. Sometimes sacrifices need to happen if you want to stay safe, Ronnie. I didn't know Jane would be here but beavers have always done things like this around here. And I loved Jane and I love you and I'm sorry we had to do this to her but I hope you understand and I want you to understand and this is all for you.

But what I say is

Oh.

Well.

I'm glad they figured it out.

Right? Aren't you glad?

RONNIE: They figured it out?

DORA: Yes. They figured it out.

And Ronnie looks scared and I walk over and reach out to her. She gives me a long look. We're staring in each other's eyes, and I have my hand out. Take my hand, Ronnie. It's going to be ok.

END OF PLAY.

www.ingramcontent.com/pod-product-compliance
Ingram Content Group UK Ltd.
Pitfield, Milton Keynes, MK11 3LW, UK
UKHW020730280225
455688UK00012B/583